The Lonely panda

RAY HUMBER

AuthorHouse™
1663 Liberty Drive
Bloomington, IN 47403
www.authorhouse.com
Phone: 1 (800) 839-8640

Published by AuthorHouse 7/27/2015

ISBN: 978-1-5049-2414-6 (sc)
ISBN: 978-1-5049-2415-3 (e)

Library of Congress Control Number: 2015911852

Print information available on the last page.

Any people depicted in stock imagery provided by Thinkstock are models,
and such images are being used for illustrative purposes only.
Certain stock imagery © Thinkstock.

This book is printed on acid-free paper.

Because of the dynamic nature of the Internet, any web addresses or links contained in this book may have changed
since publication and may no longer be valid. The views expressed in this work are solely those of the author and do not
necessarily reflect the views of the publisher, and the publisher hereby disclaims any responsibility for them.

authorHOUSE®

The Lonely
panda

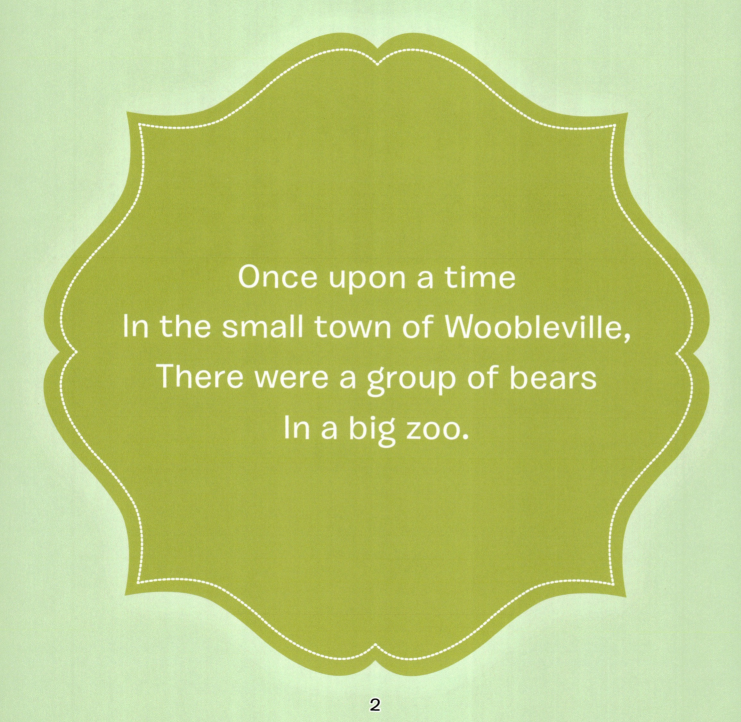

Once upon a time
In the small town of Woobleville,
There were a group of bears
In a big zoo.

All the grizzly bears
were alike.

They looked the same,
ate the same,
and talked the same way.

They all got along with each other.
No fights, or arguments,
and they all accepted one another.

One day, a new bear was added to the bear exhibit.

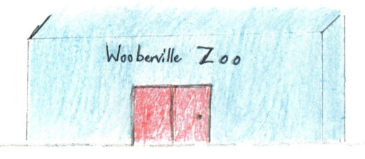

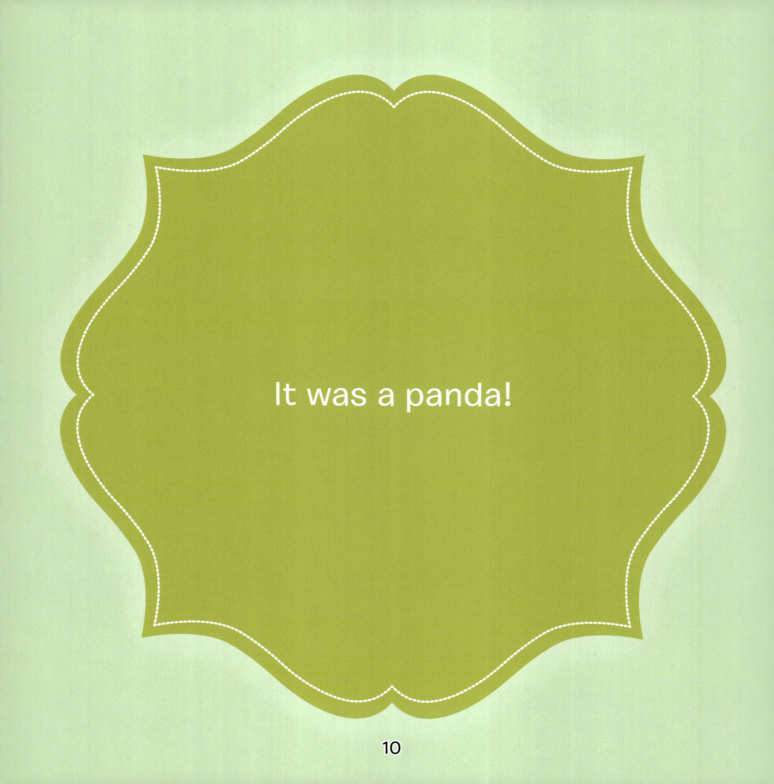

It was a panda!

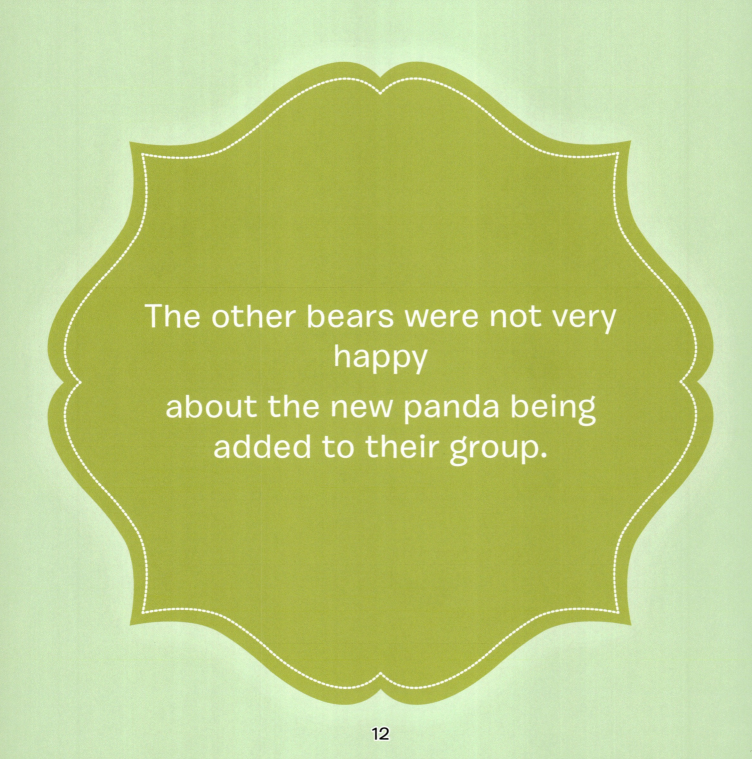

The other bears were not very happy
about the new panda being added to their group.

13

The panda decided to go
and meet the other bears.

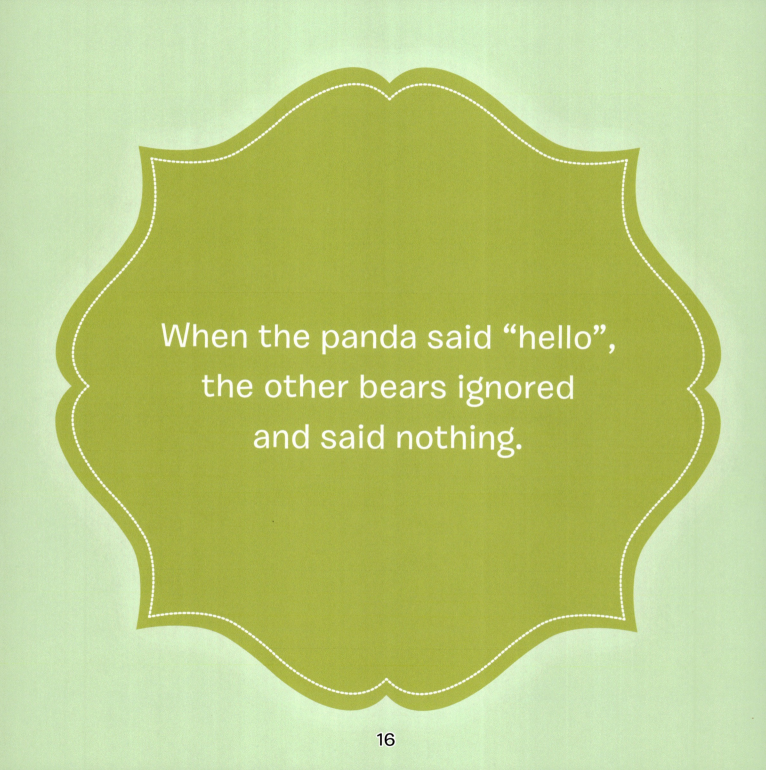

When the panda said "hello",
the other bears ignored
and said nothing.

The panda thought the other bears didn't hear him and said hello again, but the grizzly bears said nothing, and went on with their way.

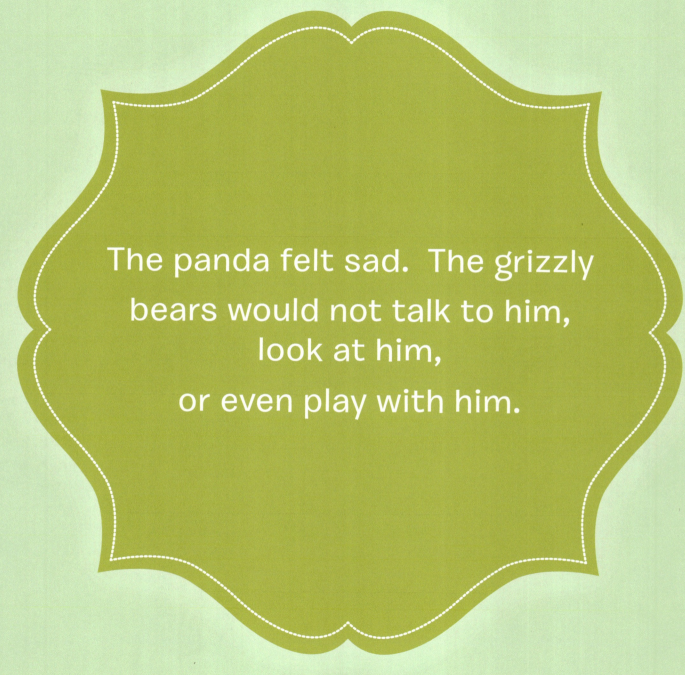

The panda felt sad. The grizzly bears would not talk to him, look at him, or even play with him.

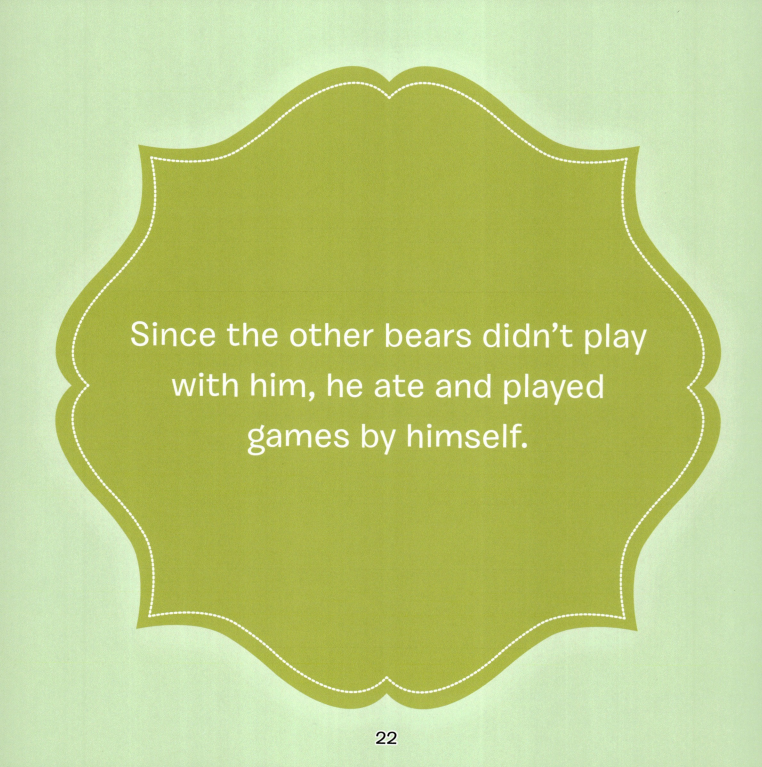

Since the other bears didn't play with him, he ate and played games by himself.

23

After a while, the panda became lonely. He felt sad and gloomy that the other bears would not include him in their games.

One day when the zoo opened, and the people went to

the bear exhibit, all of the attention went to the panda.

"That panda is adorable," one girl said.

"That panda is cute," another girl said.

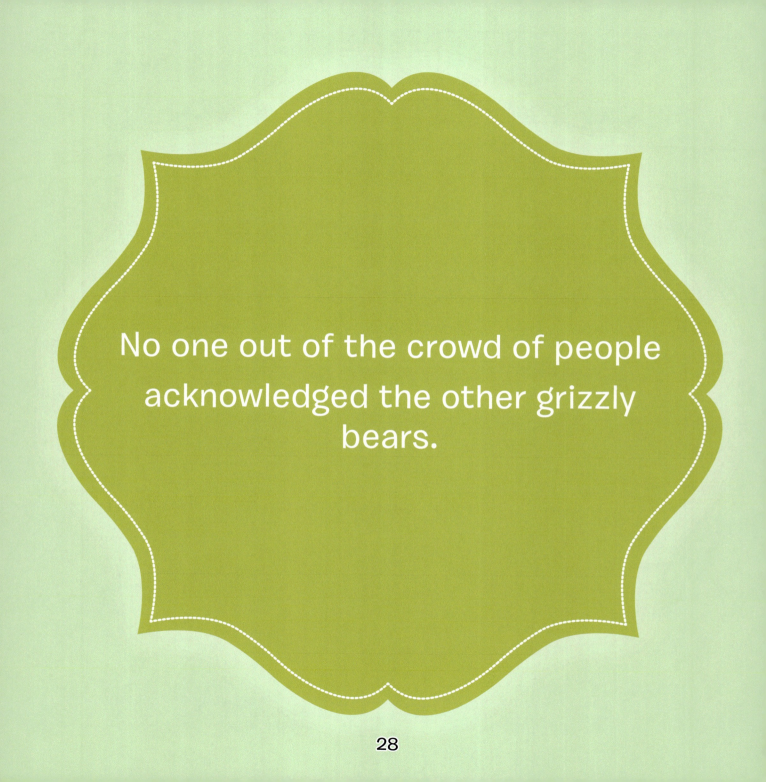

No one out of the crowd of people acknowledged the other grizzly bears.

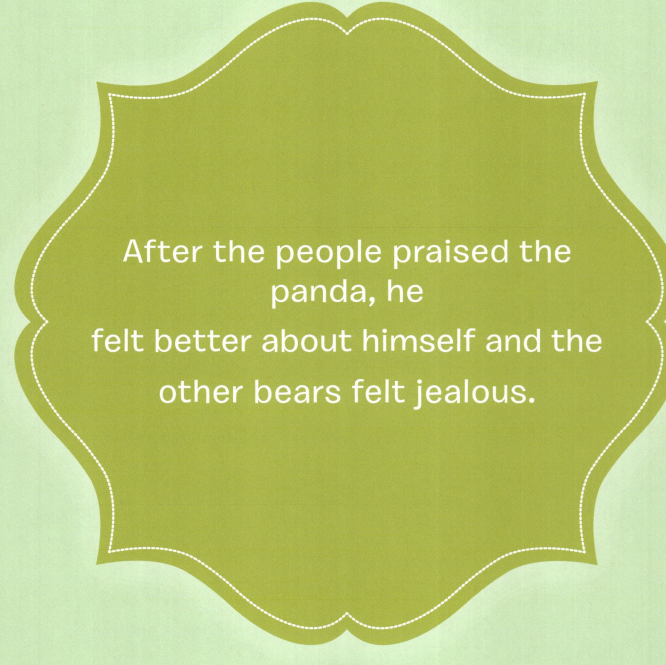

After the people praised the panda, he
felt better about himself and the
other bears felt jealous.

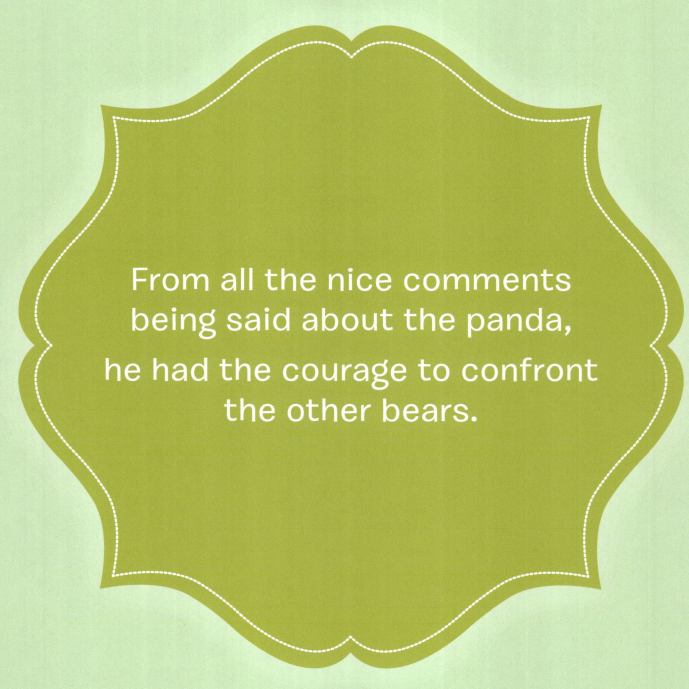

From all the nice comments being said about the panda,

he had the courage to confront the other bears.

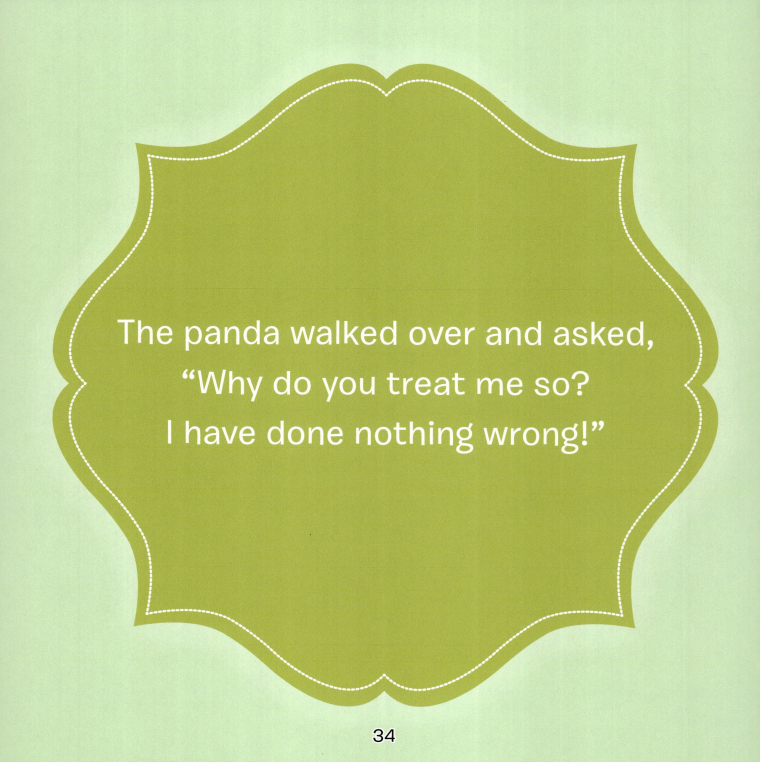

The panda walked over and asked,
"Why do you treat me so?
I have done nothing wrong!"

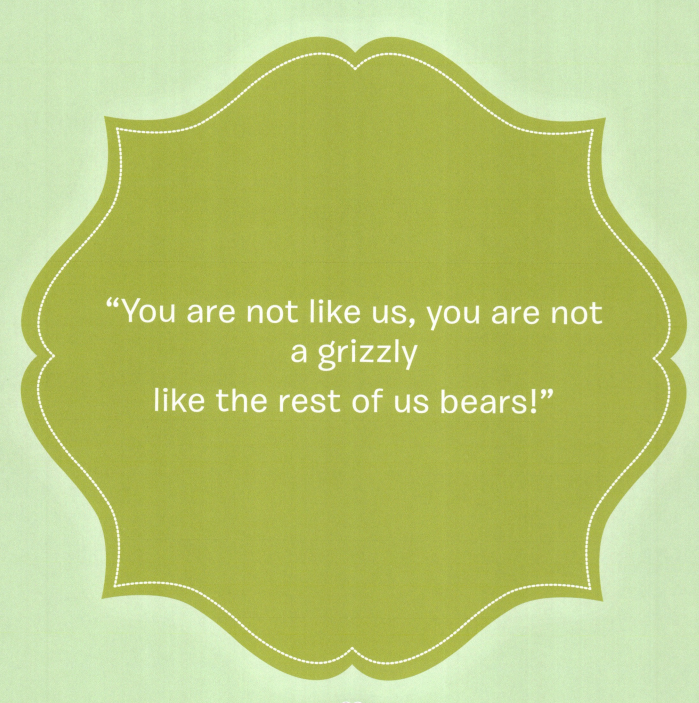

"You are not like us, you are not a grizzly

like the rest of us bears!"

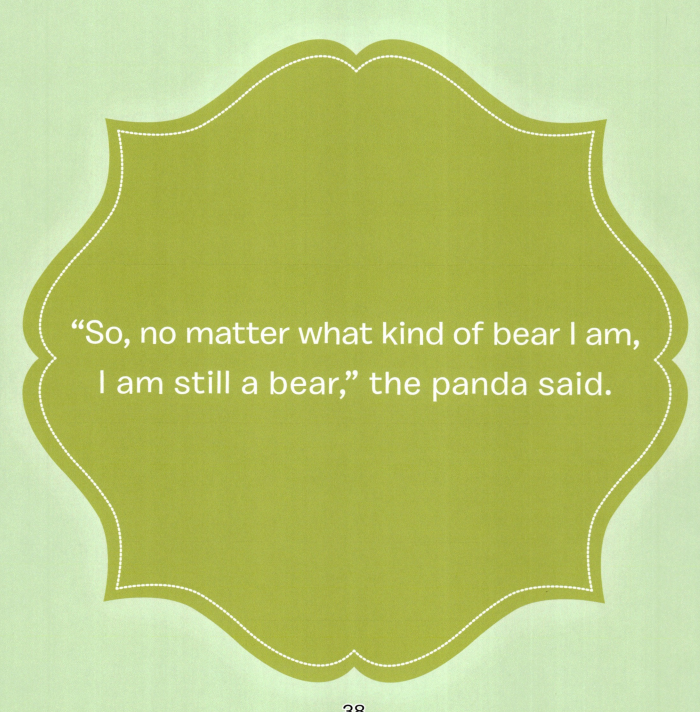

"So, no matter what kind of bear I am, I am still a bear," the panda said.

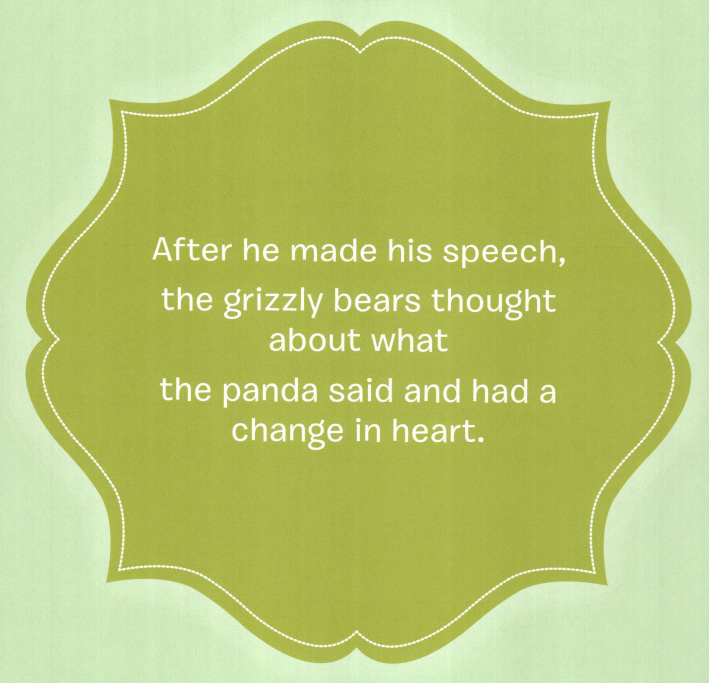

After he made his speech,
the grizzly bears thought
about what
the panda said and had a
change in heart.

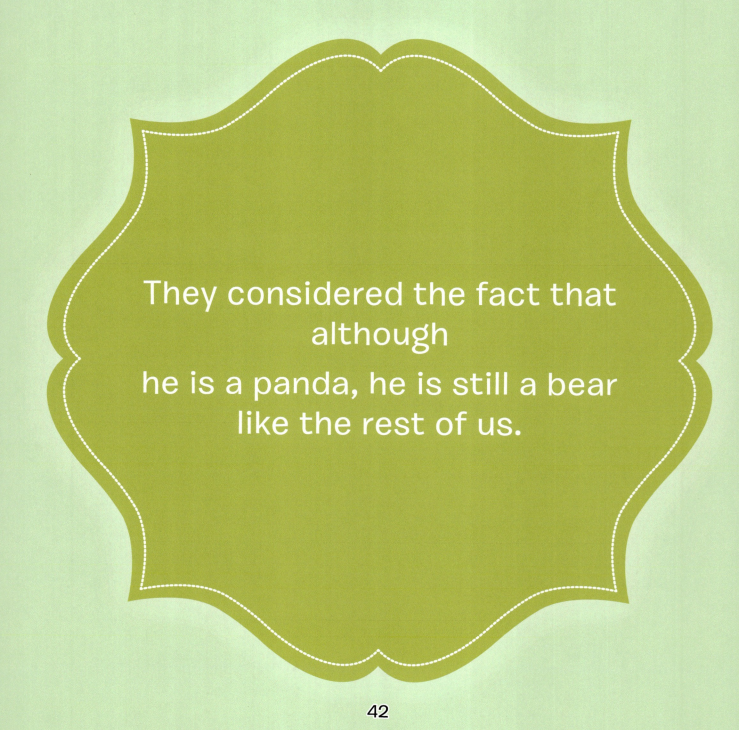

They considered the fact that although
he is a panda, he is still a bear
like the rest of us.

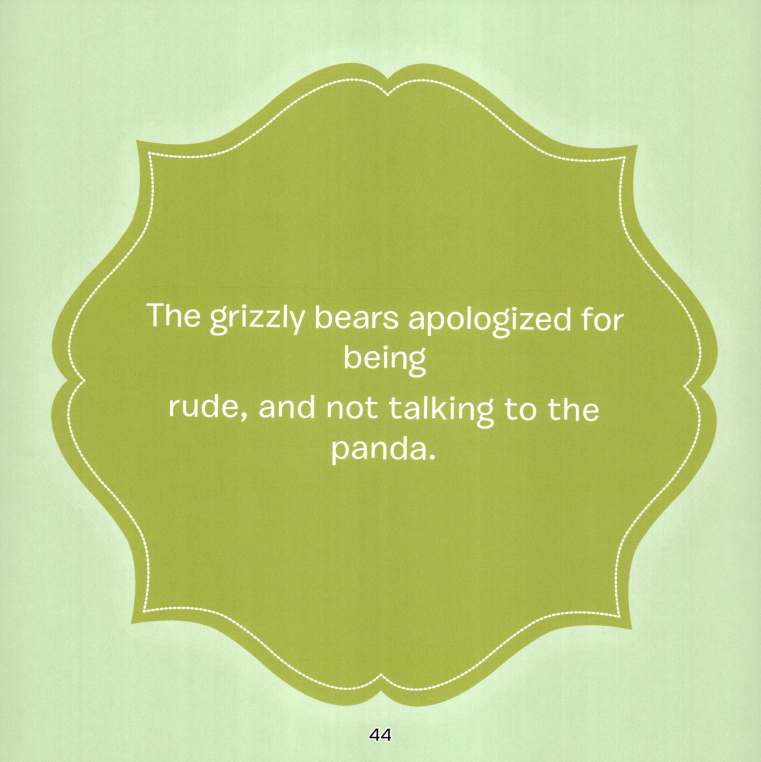

The grizzly bears apologized for being
rude, and not talking to the panda.

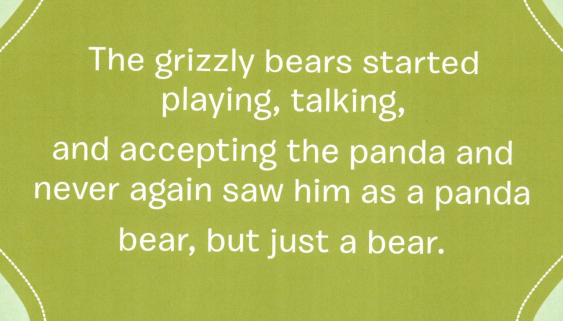

The grizzly bears started playing, talking,
and accepting the panda and never again saw him as a panda bear, but just a bear.

I Am Who I Am

I am human like everyone else
I may have a different name,
But I am who I am, a person,
And that will always remain.

You can bark, scam,
And slander against my name,
But I am who I am,
And that will not ever change.

Get your brush and paint me however you like

You can punch and kick me with all your might

Try to bring me down if that is your aim, but I am who I am,

And will forever be the same.

Say what you will, and call me out of my name

Accept me or not, and choose to be lame,

But I will not change my plan,

Because, I am who I am.

Printed in the United States
By Bookmasters